The Secret of the Sands

Written by Cynthia Rider
based on the original characters
created by Roderick Hunt and Alex Brychta
Illustrated by Alex Brychta

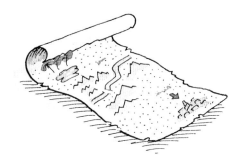

OXFORD
UNIVERSITY PRESS

The children were playing on the
computer. They were playing Chip's
new game, Secret of the Sands.

Suddenly, the magic key began to
glow. "Look at the key!" cried Biff.
"It's time for an adventure."

Floppy growled. He didn't want an adventure, but the magic was starting to work.

The magic took the children into
a desert. They saw a boy riding a
camel across the hot sands.

The boy rode up to them.

"My name is Ali," he said. "You must come to my tent. You can't stay out in this hot sun."

Ali helped the children climb onto the camels. Floppy sat with Kipper.

"This camel is too bumpy for me," thought Floppy.

Ali took the children to his tent.

He gave them some cooler clothes.

Then he showed them a map.

"I'm going to the village on this map," said Ali. "Nobody lives there now, but long ago my father hid some treasure there. He called it the Secret of the Sands."

"Secret of the Sands! That's the
same name as my game," cried
Chip. "Can we help you to find the
treasure?"

"Oh yes! I'd like you to help," said Ali. "Come on, let's go!"

They rode through deep, rocky valleys and up steep, sandy hills.

At last, they came to the village.
There was sand everywhere. It had
blown into the empty rooms and
drifted over the walls.

"There must have been a sandstorm," said Ali. "It all looks different from the map. I don't know where to look."

Wilf pointed to an old tower.

"That's the tower on the map,"
he said. "We must be very near the
treasure. Let's look here."

They looked into the shadowy
rooms and poked the sand with sticks.

"I'll help, too," thought Floppy,
and he dug some deep holes.

Suddenly, Floppy disappeared.

"Help!" shouted Biff. "Floppy has fallen down a hole. We must rescue him."

They climbed down into a hidden
room. Wilma shone her torch around
and something glittered in the light.
It was a treasure chest!

The chest was full of glittering
gold and sparkling jewels.

"The Secret of the Sands!" said Ali.
"How beautiful!"

The children put the chest onto
Ali's camel.

Suddenly, they heard a noise. It
grew louder and louder.

Two men on a motorbike came
speeding towards them.

"They're desert
robbers," cried Ali.
"They're after the
treasure!"

The children raced away but the robbers came closer and closer.

"They're going to catch us," cried Biff. "What can we do?"

Suddenly, there was a loud crash!

"Floppy has saved us!" shouted Kipper. "The robbers have fallen into one of his holes. They'll never catch us now."

They got back safely, and Ali gave
Floppy a golden camel. "Thank you
for saving us," he said.

The magic key began to glow.

"It's time for us to go," said Biff.

The magic took the children
home.

"What an adventure!" said Chip.

"What glittering gold!" said Wilma.

"What big bumpy camels!"
thought Floppy.

Talk about the story

Why do you think the book is called The Secret of the Sands?

Why didn't Floppy like the adventure?

How did Floppy save the children?

What sort of treasure would you like to find?

A maze

Help Ali find the treasure.